Snowy, Blowy Winter

Bob Raczka

Illustrated by **Judy Stead**

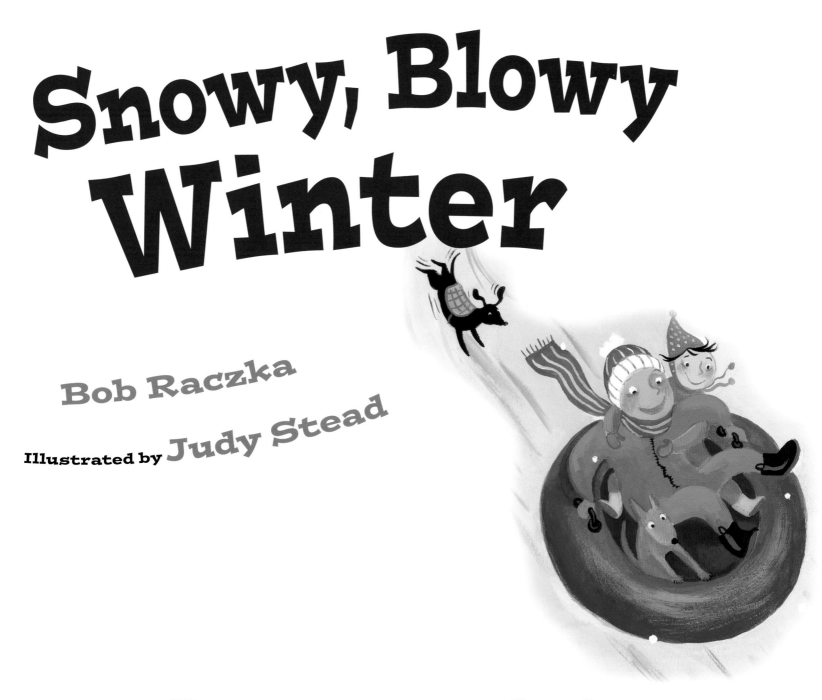

Albert Whitman & Company, Morton Grove, Illinois

Also by Bob Raczka and Judy Stead:

Spring Things

Who Loves the Fall?

Library of Congress Cataloging-in-Publication Data

Raczka, Bob.
Snowy, blowy winter / by Bob Raczka ; illustrated by Judy Stead.
p. cm.
Summary: Illustrations and simple rhyming text portray winter activities, from snowman-building, sledding, and sitting by a fire to feeding birds.
ISBN 978-0-8075-7526-0
[1. Stories in rhyme. 2. Winter—Fiction. 3. Snow—Fiction.] I. Stead, Judy, ill. II. Title.
PZ8.3.R11153Sn 2008   [E—dc22] 2007052608

The design is by Carol Gildar.

For more information about Albert Whitman & Company,
please visit our web site at www.albertwhitman.com.

To Robert, who was born in the winter and is growing up way too fast.—POPS.

To Zoe and Nicky and all the snow people we made in winters past.—J.S.

Snowy,

blowy,

windows are glowy.

Frosty,

freezy,

stuffy and sneezy.

Strappy.

zippery,

icy and slippery!

Angels are lovely.

Sidewalks are shovely.

Breathy,

nippy.

cocoa is sippy.

Rosy,

COZY.

everyone's dozy.

Messy,

gooey,

melty and chewy.

Seedy,

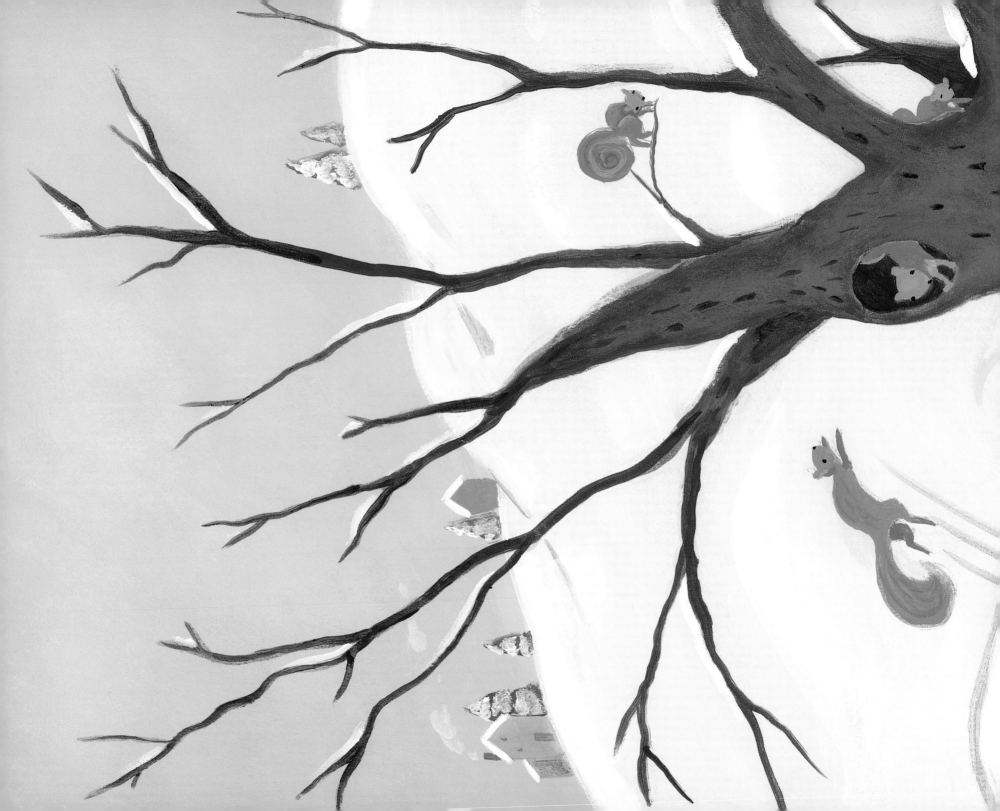

squirrelly,

will spring come early?